Foreign Exchange

a novel

george dardess

Austen Press

Manufactured in the United States of America by
AUSTEN PRESS
620 PARK AVENUE #119
ROCHESTER, NY 14607
716-271-8520
FAX 716-442-6057

Copyright © 1994 by George Dardess
All rights reserved

ISBN 0-9638052-9-0
Library of Congress Catalog Card Number 93-72785

FIRST TRADE EDITION
FIRST PUBLISHED IN 1994 BY
AUSTEN PRESS

Without limiting the rights under copyright reserved above, no part of this publication may be reproduced, stored in or introduced into a retrieval system, or transmitted, in any form or by any means (electronic, mechanical, photocopying, recording or otherwise), without the prior written permission of both the copyright owner and the above publisher of this book.

Author's Foreword

If you were living in Japan or Italy, say, and you opened a novel and saw cartoon strips, you wouldn't blink an eye. In many countries of Europe and Asia, the "graphic novel," as it's called, is a common and popular way for serious writers to tell stories. And because of this wide acceptance, artists and writers have been able to produce work of the highest sophistication and quality. One thinks of Keiji Nakazawa's *Barefoot Gen: A Cartoon Story of Hiroshima* or of Tsai Chih Chung's cartoon adaptations of the Daoist classics.

What do these artists and writers (and their readers) find so attractive about the cartoon medium? Art Spiegelman, whose graphic narrative *Maus* recently won a Pulitzer Prize, describes the genre's attractiveness this way. Graphic novels, he says, are

> as disparate from books as is a play or a movie. It's a different experience entirely. Pictures carry another kind of information than words. What is most exciting is that a picture language and a word language can interweave, which can't be done by either one alone.

Joseph Witek, author of *Comic Books as History*, makes a similar point:

> What the comic book can do which...prose alone cannot is to show in space the relations of the physical elements of the story..., and it can keep previous scenes physically before the reader after the narrative has moved on...; the images are at once more immediate and more subliminal than in prose.

At its best, say both authors, the graphic novel can combine the verbal and visual arts in one expressive medium. The strength of words lies in their abstraction, their ability to convey ideas. The strength of pictures lies in their concreteness, their ability to shape our perception of particular things. Together, words and pictures give immediacy to ideas and generality to what we see.

The cartoon medium has another special strength, too: the capacity to present our conflict with the physical or animal side of our nature. Unlike fables, which tend to present this conflict moralistically, cartoons treat the gap between our human presumptions and our animalness in a comic way, emphasizing incongruity, absurdity, fantasy, anarchy, human solidarity (because we are all shown to be limited beings always overstepping ourselves, continually falling on our faces or slipping on banana peels). Mickey Mouse is amusing, not because he is a mouse, but because he is a mouse behaving in some of the silly ways in which we behave.

But silliness doesn't tell the whole story of our behavior. Mickey's least humanlike trait isn't his big ears or his long tail. It's his lack of a tragic dimension. The absence of this dimension in Mickey limits his appeal and seriousness. He can only be "cute." And just as Mickey has been limited, so has the American cartoon environment which he grew up in and came to define. It too has been limited by its emphasis on cuteness and superficial humor. No wonder that efforts to convince the American public of the medium's serious potential have often been met by scepticism.

Art Spiegelman's *Maus*, mentioned earlier, may have changed all that. Spiegelman's decision to portray the Jews at Auschwitz as mice and the Nazis as cats freed Mickey from his infantilism. Mickey has now reached maturity, and so has (one hopes) the American cartoon environment as well.

FOREIGN EXCHANGE, unlike *Maus*, is a fiction. (*Maus* is Spiegelman's account of his relationship with his father, a Holocaust survivor.) But FOREIGN EXCHANGE is like *Maus* in taking the cartoon medium seriously, using it to tell a story in which characters develop as they do in classic novel and drama forms. The main characters, of diverse ethnic backgrounds, are subjected to forces that change them in painful but positive ways, so that they become more fully human than they were at the beginning. They become more understanding of themselves and more aware of the responsibility they share in bringing about each other's misery and happiness.

The reader/viewer of FOREIGN EXCHANGE is invited to discover for herself or himself the various levels of meaning implicit in the novel's title. My hope is that the title will come also to have an added meaning: that FOREIGN EXCHANGE will join *Maus*—and other existing and future graphic novels by Americans—in helping to bring the serious cartoon narrative home, where it began. As publisher Byron Preiss notes:

> Comics are the jazz of the printed word. Like jazz, it's a native American art form that gained its true popularity abroad. Europe and Japan preserved the medium when it waned here, and now we see it coming back to us.

Contents

Part One	Enter Rudi	
	Chapter 1	3
Part Two	Rudi at School	
	Chapter 2	15
	Chapter 3	24
	Chapter 4	35
	Chapter 5	43
Part Three	Rudi's Hit	
	Chapter 6	53
	Chapter 7	63
Part Four	Rudi's Rise	
	Chapter 8	75
	Chapter 9	86
	Chapter 10	95
Part Five	Rudi's Fall	
	Chapter 11	109
	Chapter 12	116
	Chapter 13	125
Epilogue	Rudi's Legacy	
	Chapter 14	137

Part One

Enter Rudi

Chapter 1

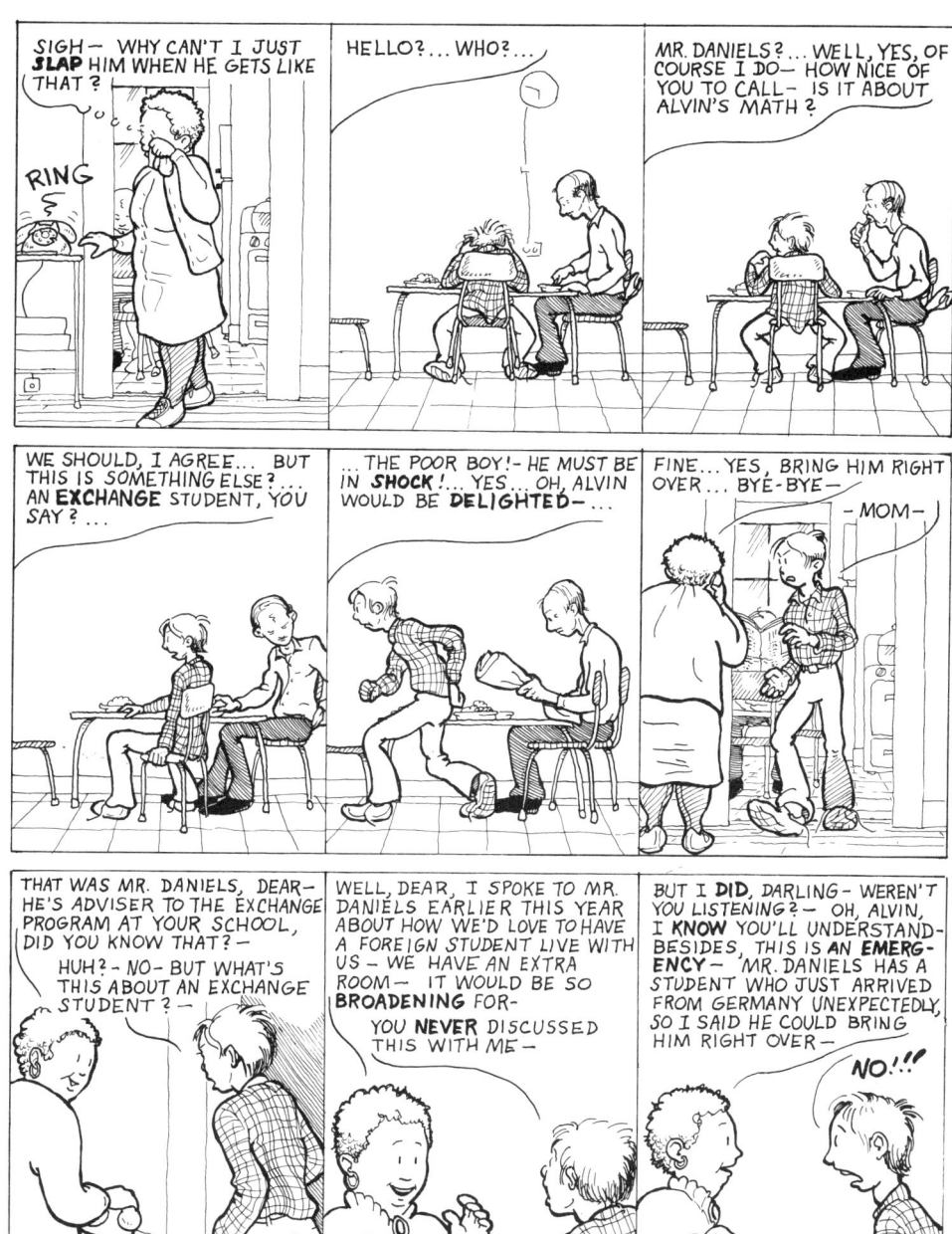

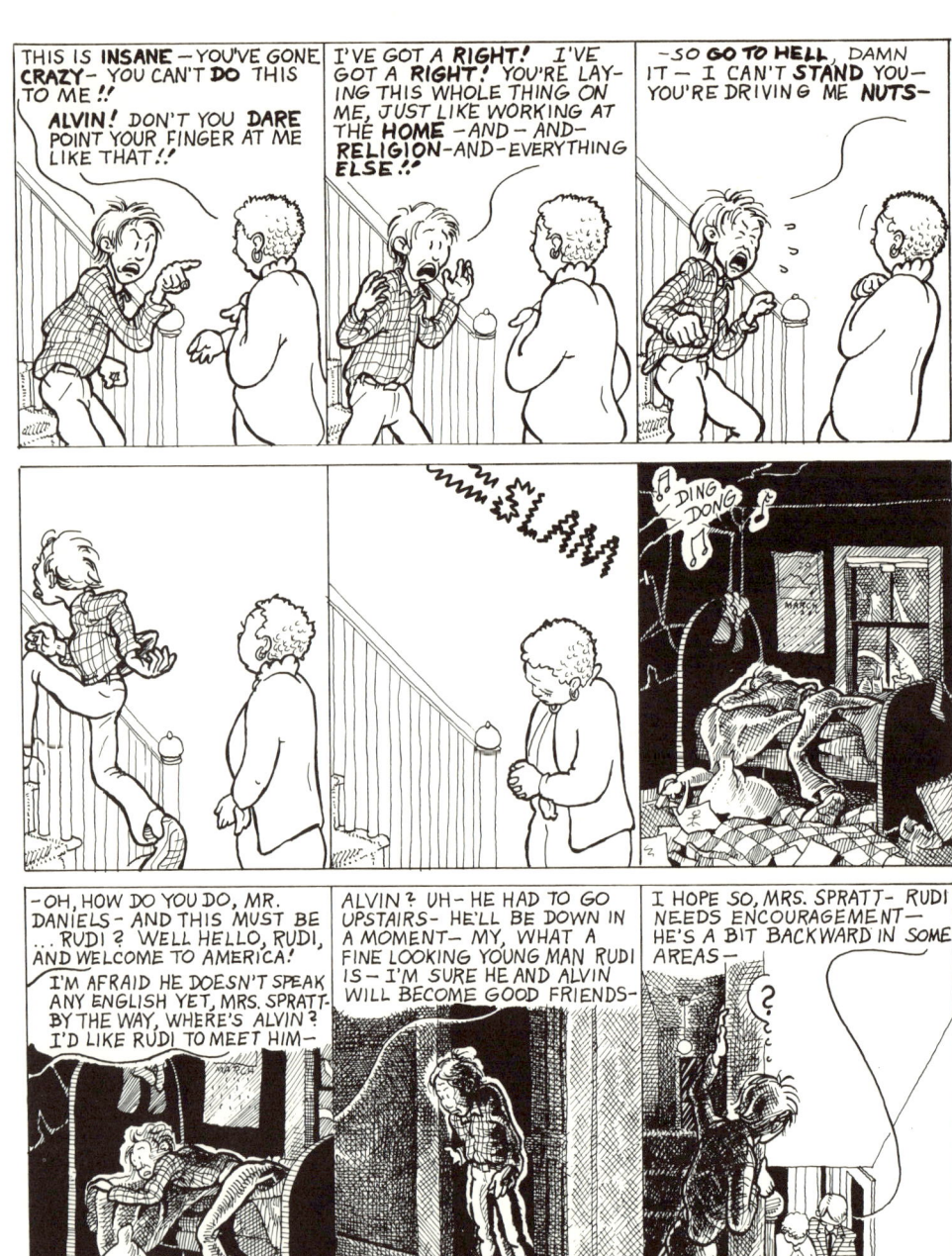

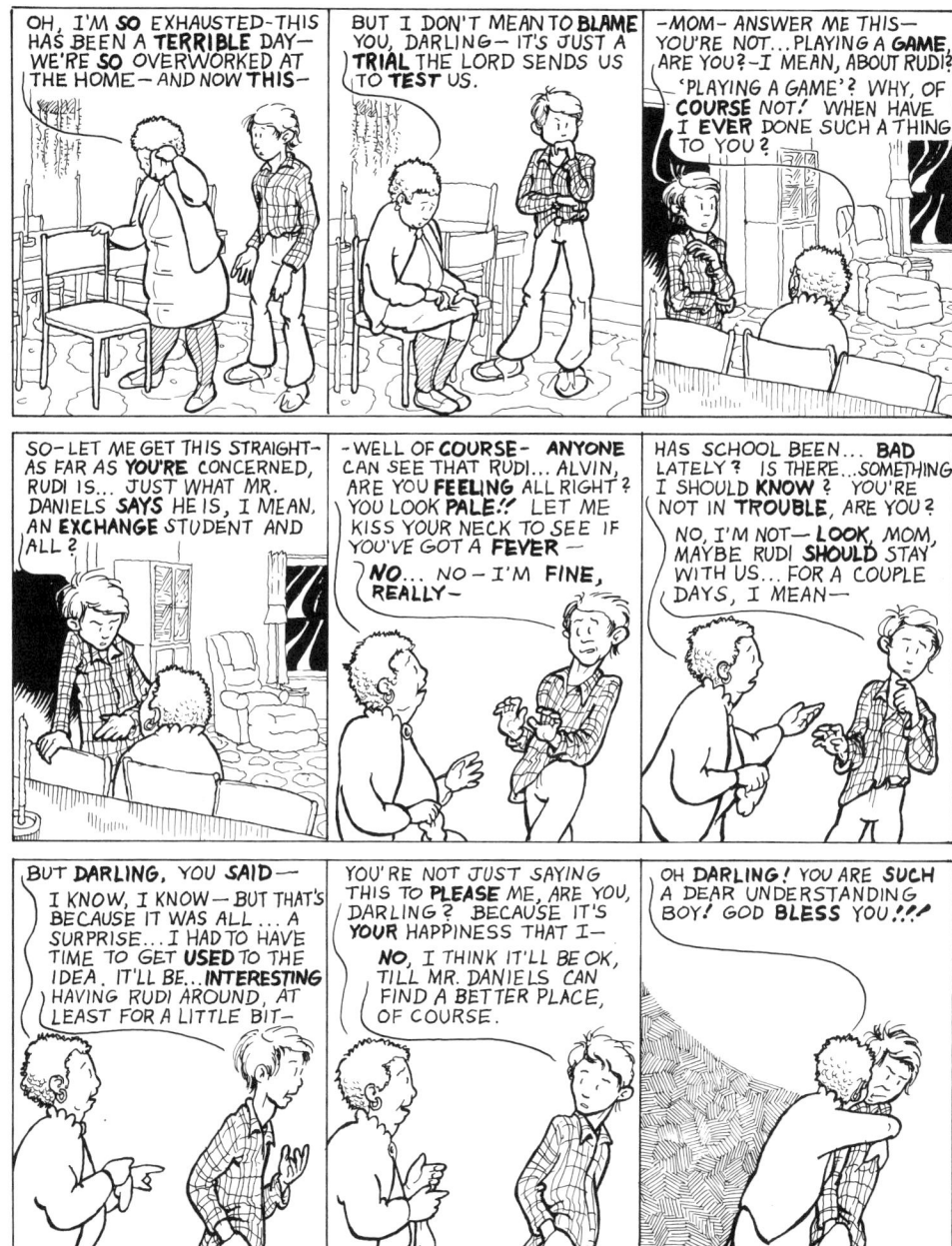

Part Two

Rudi at School

Chapter 2

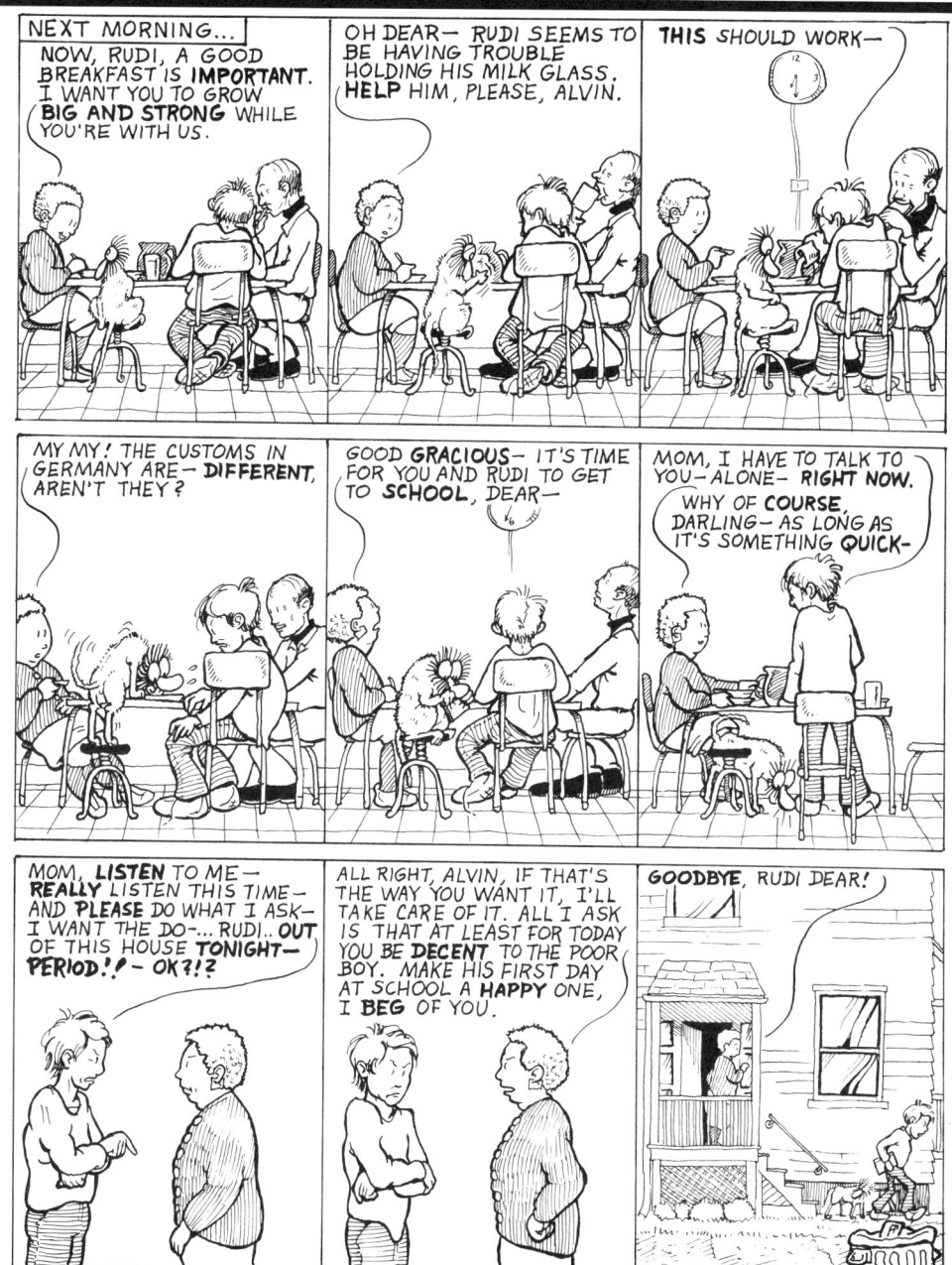

Chapter 3

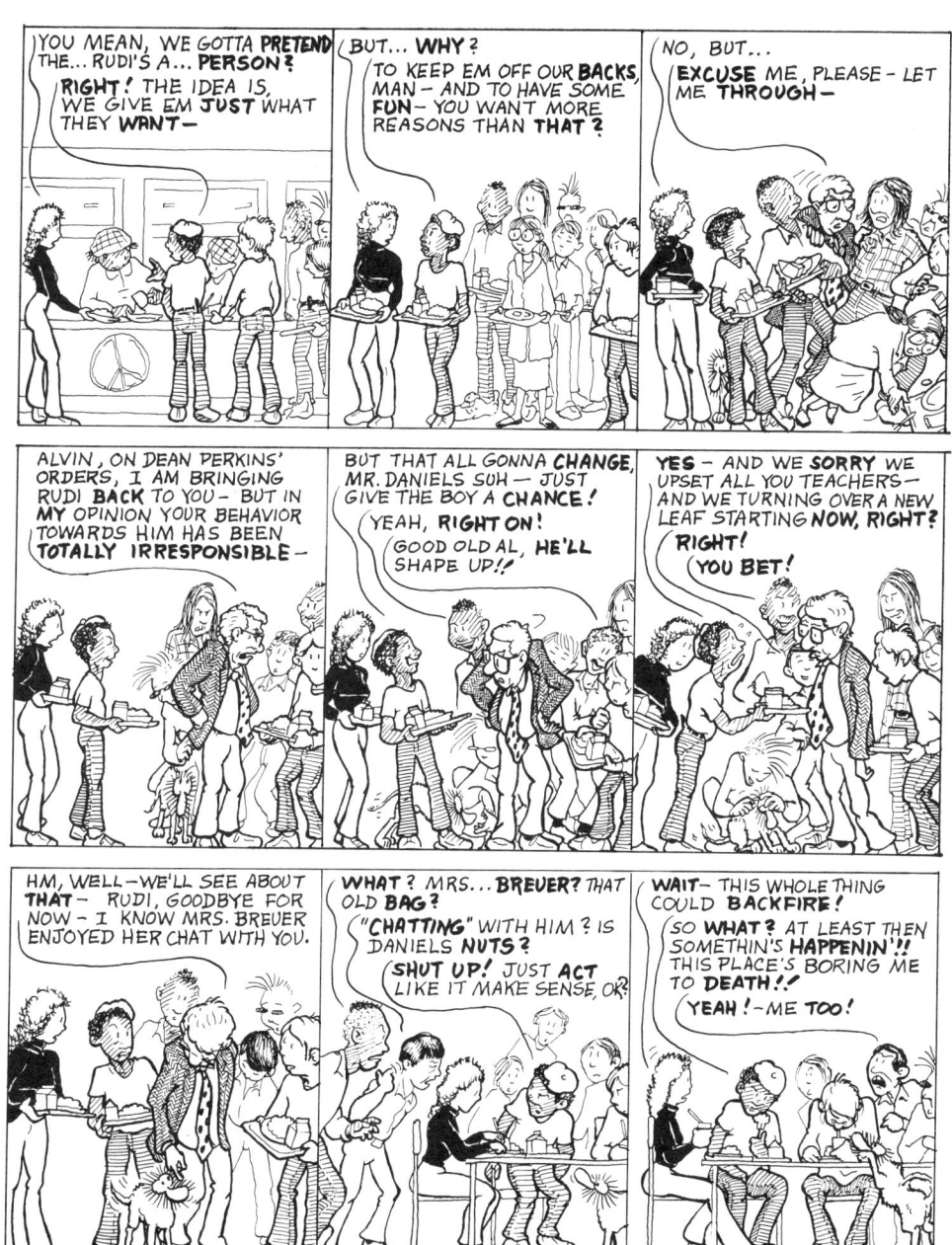

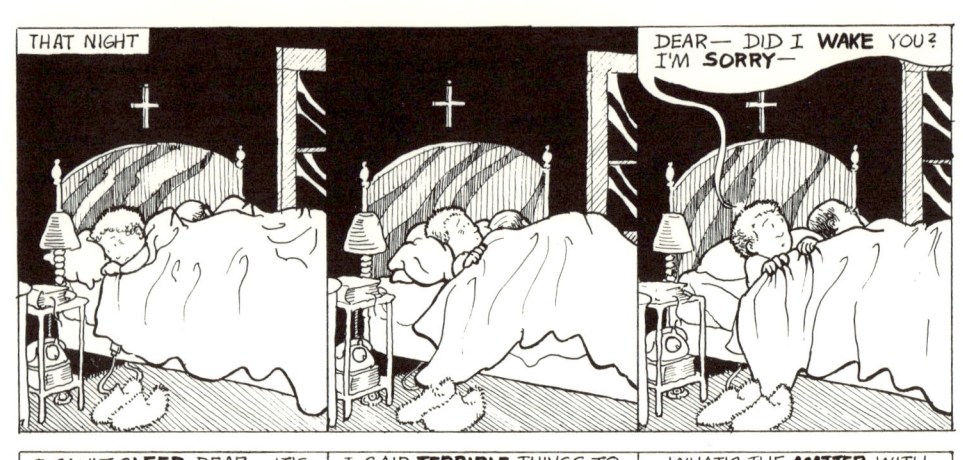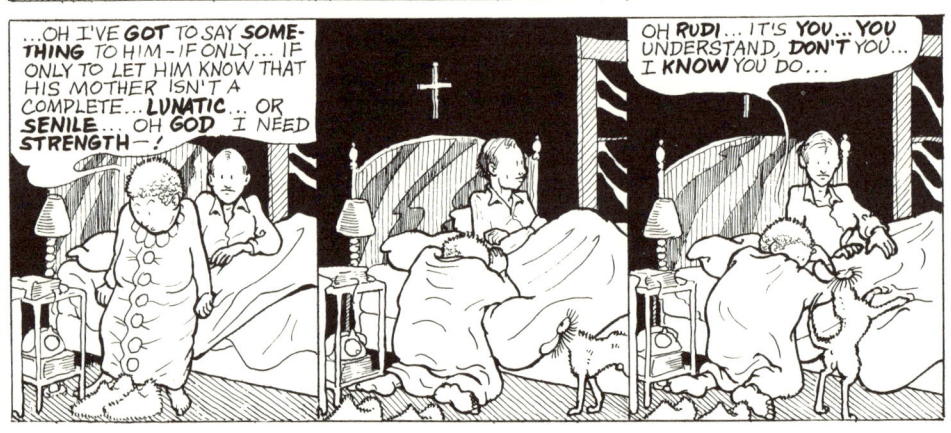

Chapter 4

Chapter 5

Part Three

Rudi's Hit

Chapter 6

Chapter 7

Part Four

Rudi's Rise

Chapter 8

Chapter 9

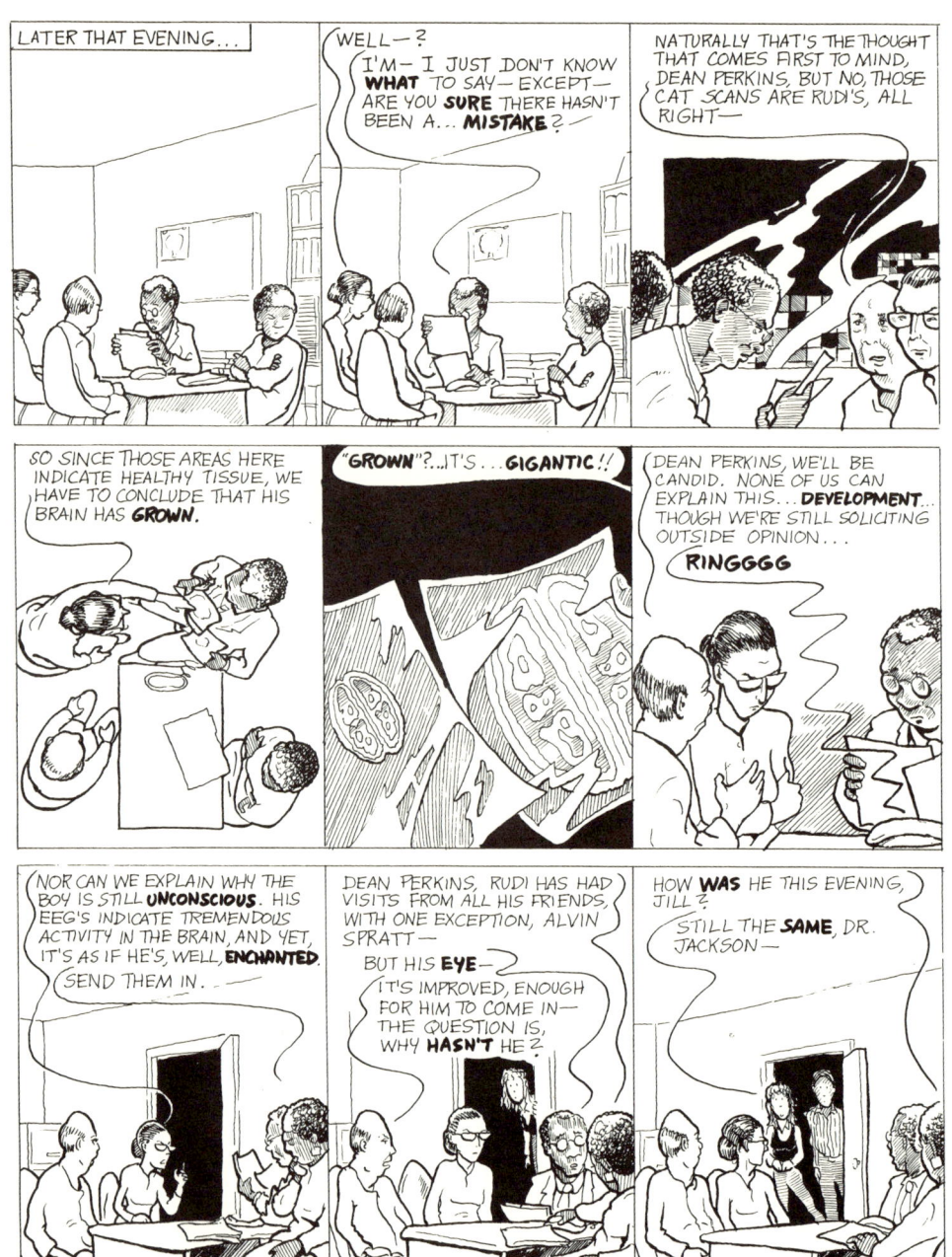

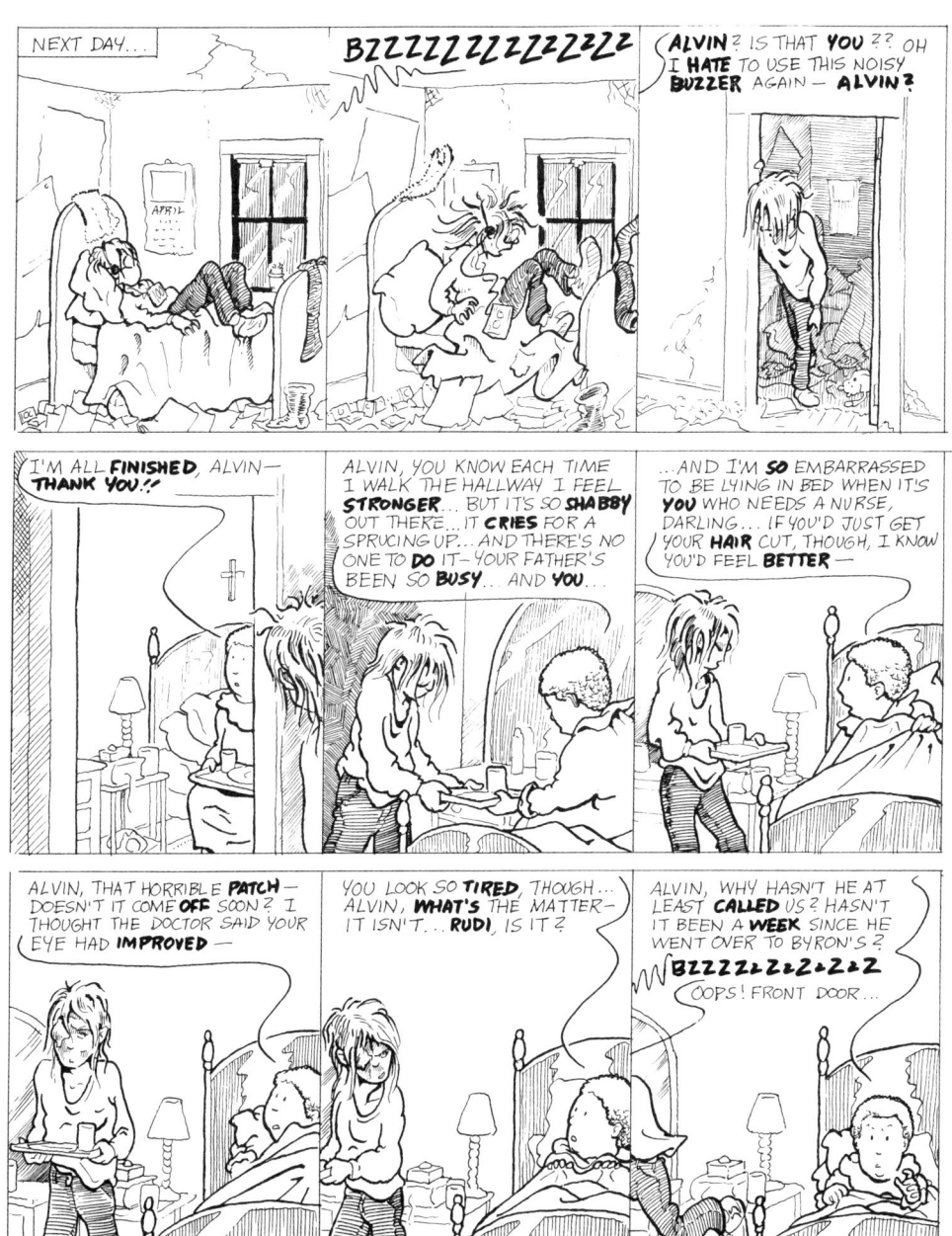

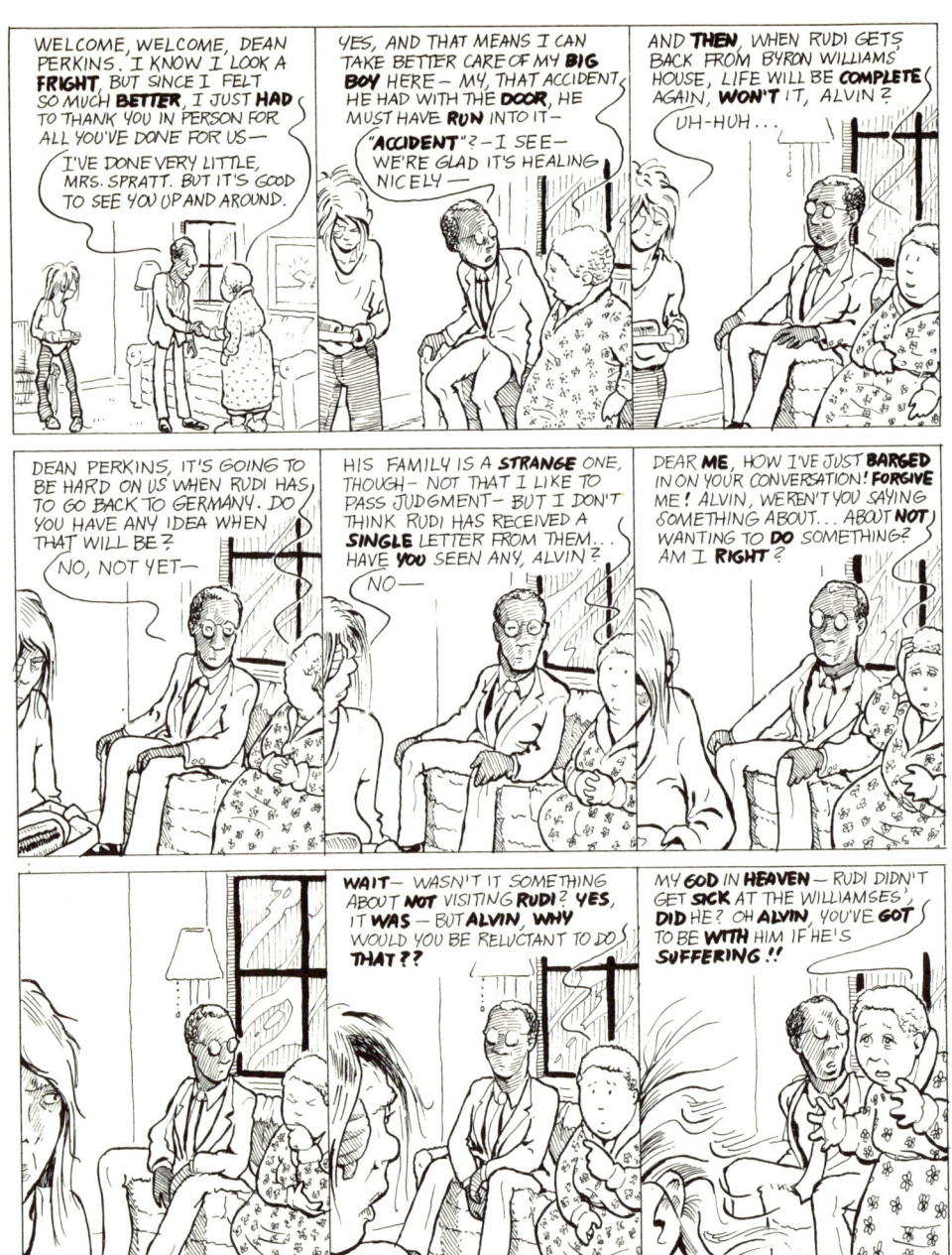

Chapter 10

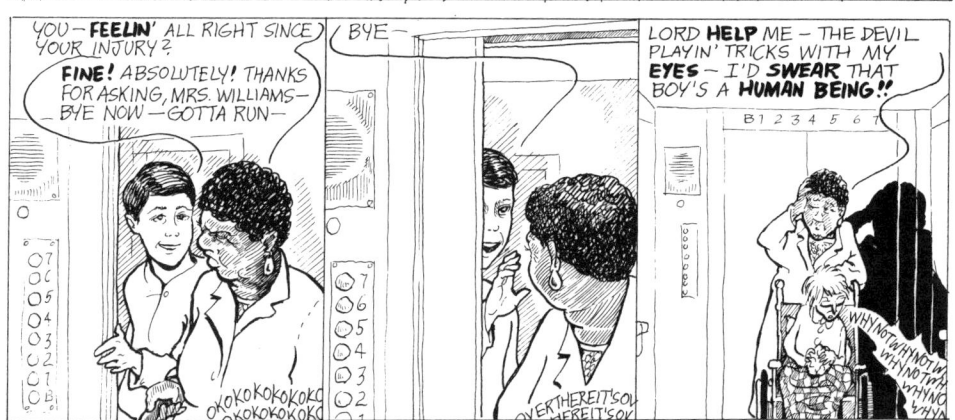

Part Five

Rudi's Fall

Chapter 11

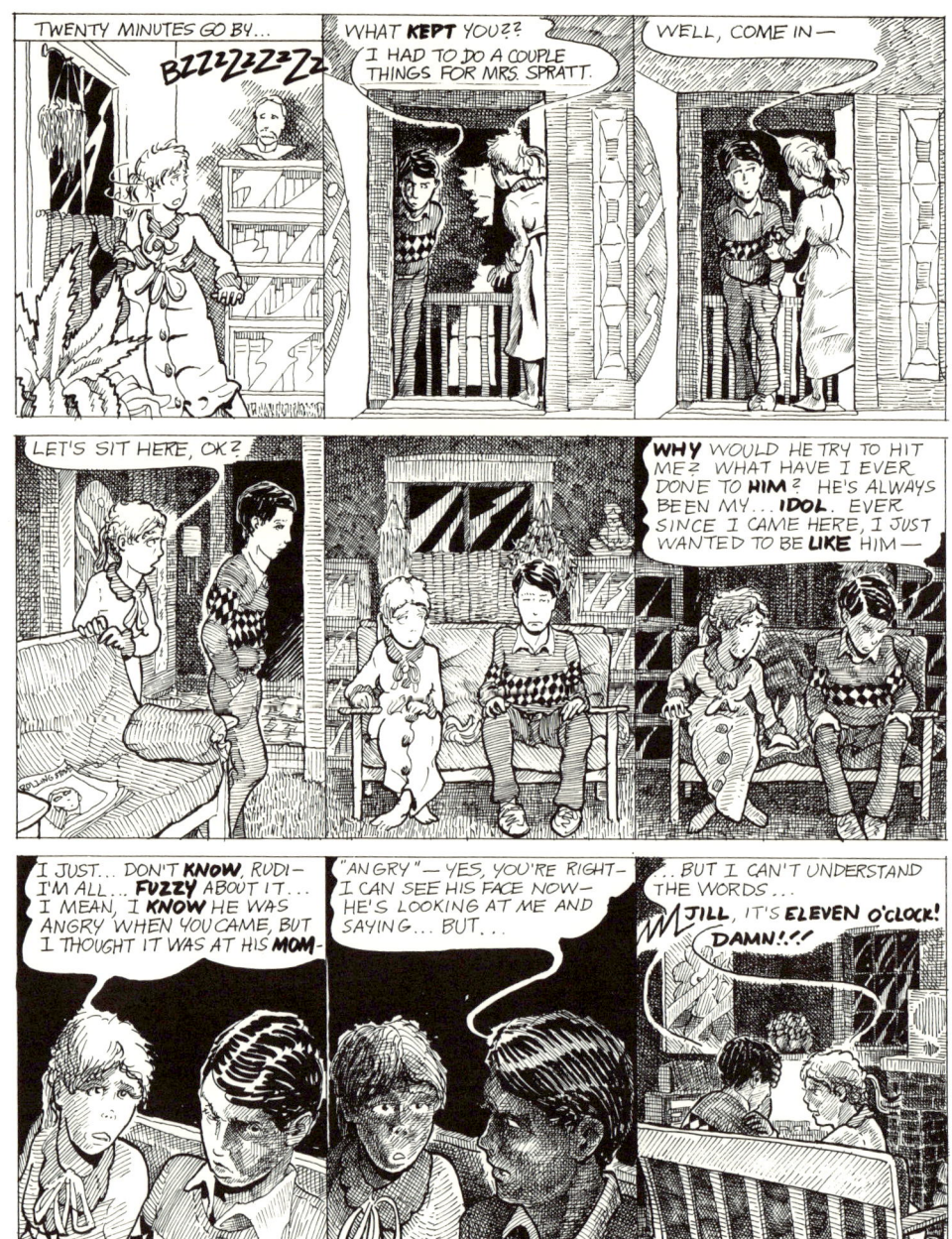

Chapter 12

Chapter 13

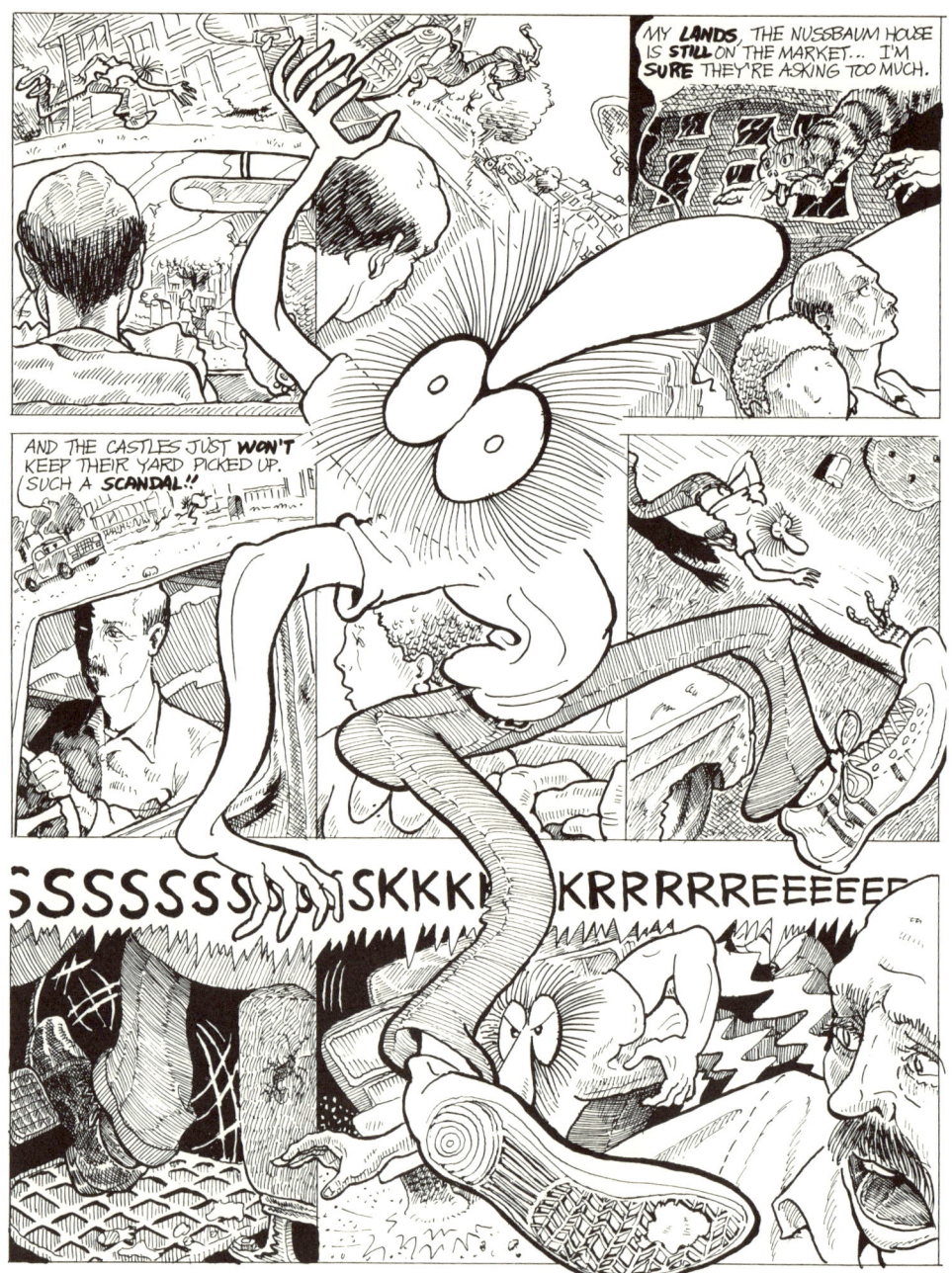

Epilogue

Rudi's Legacy

Chapter 14

137

About the Author

George Dardess is the illustrator of a cartoon interpretation of Whitman's "Song of Myself," author of several articles on Jack Kerouac, and co-author of *Every Cliché in the Book*. He has taught literature at Rutgers and Tufts Universities and is currently High School English Department Chair at Allendale Columbia School.

DATE DUE

FEB 17 2011			
GAYLORD			PRINTED IN U.S.A.

LAKE PARK HIGH SCHOOL RESOURCE CENTER ROSELLE, IL 60172